Printed in China

The type was set in Univers.

The illustrations were created using pencil and mixed media.

Library of Congress Cataloging-in-Publication Data

Saxton, Patricia.
A book of fairies / Patricia Saxton.
    p. cm.
Summary: A handbook on the habitat, language, magic, and everyday life of fairies, including how to please them.

ISBN 978-1-934860-01-4

[1. Fairies--Fiction.] I. Title.
PZ7.S27438Bo 2009
[E]--dc22

2009003215

For my mother, my sister Anne, and my daughter Carolyn

a book of fairies

patricia saxton

fairies love roses for their scent and
their beauty. If you would like fairies
to feel welcome, plant roses in your
garden... They also adore
bluebells!

DAWN, DUSK, & MIDNIGHT

Best times to glimpse a fairy

If you listen carefully,
you might hear fairies'
laughter and songs

FAIRY RINGS —
MUSHROOM CIRCLES
DON'T STEP INSIDE THEM!
You may start dancing
with the fairies and not
be able to stop. A friend
may have to pull you out.

a book of fairies

fair·y (fâr'e)
n. **pl.** fair·ies
A tiny being in human form, clever, playful and possessing magical powers; guardian of nature, with a soft spot for children, animals and chocolate.

[also fairie, faerie, faery, fay, fey, fae; collectively, wee folk, fair folk]

—**Synonyms** 1. brownie, pixie, sprite. Fairy is the most common name: *A good fairy helped your flowers grow tall; A mischievous fairy hid my shoes.* A brownie is known for its good nature, and generally appears at night to do household tasks: *Perhaps the brownies will come and tidy the kitchen tonight.* Sprite suggests a fairy with a pleasing, child-like appearance, admired for lightness of movement: *She's as agile as a little sprite.* Pixies are especially cheerful and impish: *I do believe a pixie has led us*

Fairyland

Fairies live in what's often called Fairyland – a place that some people think is imaginary. But of course it isn't imaginary at all. It's really quite real.

You see, there's our world – the one where we eat breakfast and go to school and play basketball – and there's the magical world where fairies live. The two worlds are only separated by a hidden veil – a kind of invisible door that may look like a patch of fog or a flicker of light.

So if you dare to believe, and step through that invisible veil, you will find yourself in an entirely new place alive with mystical creatures, fairy dust and magic.

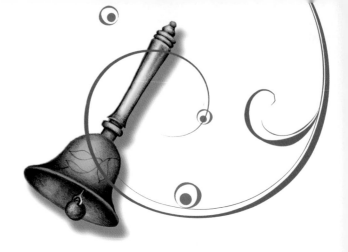

Sometimes you hear fairies before you see them – a whisper, a giggle, a faint sound of chattering or the tinkling of bells.

Finding Fairies

Fairies live and play all around us. They're in our gardens, in our woods and sometimes even in our homes. They're beside us all the time – right in front of our eyes ... even though we may not see them.

Children can see fairies quite easily – perhaps because, like fairies, they themselves are open-hearted and their heads aren't filled with grown-up nonsense that keeps them from seeing what's really there. That's why when a baby giggles and smiles and there's no one around, chances are they're looking at a fairy.

"I do believe in fairies.   I do! I do!!"

"I DO BELIEVE IN FAIRIES.   I DO! I DO!!"

"I do believe in fairies.   I do! I do!!"

~ Peter Pan

4

When the subject of fairies comes up in conversation, there are some adults who'll say things like "don't fill your head with such silliness," or, "isn't that cute, he thinks there really are fairies!" But don't be fooled by these remarks. They've just forgotten, the poor things.

One of the best ways to find fairies is to go to their favorite places: the edge of a stream, in the hollow of an old tree, or in their number one hide-and-seek spot, the flower garden. Just remember to be very quiet so you don't frighten them away.

If you're lucky, a tiny fairy face may peer up at you from inside a flower. Since most fairies move very quickly, it can happen in the blink of an eye. You might catch a glimpse of a leg or wing hiding behind a mushroom, resting on a tree branch, or even sitting on a shelf near your favorite book. And if you're reading a really good bedtime story, a fairy just might sit on your pillow to have a listen.

Famous Fairies

Tinkerbell: Peter Pan's friend in Never Never Land, known to be spirited, precocious and naughty

Sugar Plum Fairy: A hard-worker, and rarely seen, best known for her starring role in "The Nutcracker"

Titania: Queen of the fairies, Oberon's wife

Oberon: Fairy King, Titania's husband

Puck: Shakespeare's most mischievous fairy; also known as Robin Goodfellow

Tooth Fairy: Guardian of children's teeth

Fairy Godmother: Although made famous by Cinderella, she's really a guardian angel, and everyone has one.

Cottingley Fairies: Around 1920, the highly respected author Sir Arthur Conan Doyle was convinced that photographs of fairies taken by two young English girls were real. When the girls reached old age, they finally admitted that the pictures were faked – but they held true to their belief that they had indeed seen the fairies.

Flora, Fauna, and Merryweather: The three good fairies in "Sleeping Beauty"

Maleficent: The evil fairy in "Sleeping Beauty"

Sometimes, especially in the evening, fairies look like tiny glowing lights or small shining balls floating in the air. On a hot June night you could easily mistake their sparkling light for a firefly.

Fairies are also great shapeshifters. They can take on the form of any animal or plant. But in their natural state, when they're not hiding from enemies, they appear to be tiny, human-like creatures, usually with wings.

"Just living is not enough," said the butterfly fairy,
"one must have sunshine, freedom and a little flower."

– Hans Christian Andersen, *The Butterfly*

If you have a garden where you live, fairies might be right outside your own door. A sure sign of fairies being around is a garden that's colorful, happy and hearty.

Most of the time, though, you'll hear a fairy before you see one – a whisper, a giggle, the faint sound of chattering or the tinkling of bells. You might also hear a "whoosh!" and a fluttering of wings, and think it's a bird.

Now there's no guarantee that if you look for a fairy you'll find one. You could search high and low in your flower patch, explore every nook and cranny of the woods, and scour the stream banks hoping like mad to spot some wee folk, and never see a single one. But then again – you might!

Remember that not seeing a fairy doesn't mean they're not there ... so don't feel badly if you don't see one!

What Fairies Do

A job that fairies take very seriously is their role as nature's caretakers. They paint delicate designs on butterflies and change the color of autumn leaves. They help lost animals find their way, fix broken wings and carry fallen baby birds back to their nests. When a new fawn is born, they sprinkle it with fairy dust so its white spots appear. After it rains, they paint rainbows in the sky.

If a garden is unusually thick and luscious – loaded with dazzling flowers that bloom the brightest purples, reddest reds and yellowest yellows – you can be sure it's not just because of some fancy new fertilizer, but from a good dose of fairy dust! The garden's human caretaker, sometimes said to have a "green thumb," probably wouldn't know he'd been secretly helped by a fairy.

...inders that we are light and can reflect... ...to do so. "Let there be light" is the divine prom... ...on as a force within your life. They help you... ...wn light to shine in a new vision.

FAIRY DUST

Now if you happen to make friends with a fairy or two, here's what they might do for you. Sometimes they'll tap on your window in the middle of the night and wake you, because they want you to see how beautifully the stars are twinkling. Then they'll sprinkle you with fairy dust so you'll go right back to sleep. And in the morning you'll probably think it was all a dream.

Fairies can also help you find things. Like your lost blue socks or some coins that might have slipped under a chair cushion, or that homework you just couldn't find!

"Hand in hand,
with Fairy Grace,
will we sing,
and bless this place."

~ William Shakespeare
A Midsummer Night's Dream

SIGNS THAT FAIRIES MAY BE NEAR:

1. uncontrollable giggles for no reason
2. very lush gardens and healthy houseplants
3. flowers that bloom bigger and longer
4. pets chasing something invisible
5. tiny colored lights, or tiny white lights
6. small glowing globes in the air
7. feeling a tickle on your arm, tummy or neck
8. mushrooms growing in a full circle
9. sound of chimes or tinkling bell
10. great new ideas come to mind

Keep in mind, though, fairies can be a little bit mischievous. They'll switch your lights on and off, hide your TV remote or start your dog barking. And just like you, they *love* chocolate, so they'll be tempted to nibble a bit of yours!

Yet for every stolen treat, they'll repay you by leaving a small treasure by your door – like acorns, pinecones and polished stones, or a tiny bunch of wildflowers. Except for the Tooth Fairy, they generally don't give away money. But they do give away smiles and laughter, and extra dashes of courage just when you need it.

Like angels, fairies are not often visible to the human eye. Also like angels, fairies can be enormously helpful to humans. But unlike angels, they can be precocious and mischievous, enjoying a prank or two.

15

"Well, now that we have seen each other,' said the unicorn, 'if you'll believe in me, I'll believe in you.'"
~ Lewis Carroll
Through the Looking Glass

16

Fairy Communities

Fairyland is made of four communities of magical beings whose powers come from the elements of earth, air, water and fire. Established long, long ago, these communities depend on each other and work together in a spirit of friendly cooperation. But that's not to say there isn't the occasional disagreement!

To help keep order, a Fairy King and Fairy Queen reign over each community. The king and queen act as a team to set the rules, keep up with planetary changes, and when needed, settle clashes between elements.

Earth Fairies

Because we human beings are earthbound, earth fairies are the ones we know best. They exist in many different forms and have many different names, like pixies, elves, trolls, leprechauns and unicorns, to name a few.

But of all the earth fairies, flower fairies are around us the most. Flower fairies are the ones skipping through the ivy, or tending your vegetable patch – yet they can be awfully hard to spot. They make their clothing from leaves and colorful flower petals, so they blend right into the gardens where they play. They also like to disguise themselves as butterflies or dragonflies, which is why you might miss them if you don't look very closely!

"Wherever is love and loyalty, great purposes and lofty souls, even though in a hovel or a mine, there is fairyland."

– Charles Kingsley, *Westward Ho!*

19

Air fairies are known to
whisper inspirational secrets in the wind
to artists, writers and musicians

Air Fairies

Air fairies are part of the wind itself, glowing silver, purple or blue beneath their large, slender wings.

Some are as small as your hand and love tumbling around with falling leaves on an autumn day. Sometimes they'll slip inside your home to bask in the steam rising from a cup of hot cocoa or spread the smell of fresh-baked cookies throughout your house.

Others are very tall – two or three times your size! From high in the sky, their great fanning wings send cool breezes down to earth on a too-hot summer's day. They also spread seeds, keep migrating birds on their path and fill the air with the sweet sound of wind chimes.

"The fairy poet takes a sheet of moonbeam, silver white; His ink is dew from daisies sweet, His pen a point of light."

~ Joyce Kilmer, *In Fairyland*

Water Fairies

Water fairies conjure up ripples in quiet streams, and great frosty waves in the sea. They live wherever there is water – in lakes, rivers, creeks, waterfalls, marshlands and oceans. You can find them under lily pads, hiding in seashells, dancing in water fountains. You can even find them in the rain!

Like Mermaids, water fairies have especially beautiful voices, and their songs have been said to cast magical spells. If you're not feeling well, their strong healing powers can help you feel better and their sweet, soothing voices can lull you to sleep.

WHAT FAIRIES MOST LOVE:
Lush, wild gardens
Animals
Children
Bright shiny glittery things
Sweet treats
Sunshine
Laughter
Practical Jokes
Playing
Little houses made of sticks
and mud and leaves, with lots
of windows and floors
Art, music and dancing
Bubbles

23

Fire Fairies

If you watch carefully, you can see fire fairies dancing in the flames of a campfire, their tiny bright sparks rising up into the summer night. But beware, their tempers burn hot. If you try to trap them in a jar, their anger can flare up and burn you!

The most courageous and powerful fairies in Fairyland, fire fairies can cause lightening to strike, make volcanoes erupt and even cause solar eclipses. In ancient times, they supplied fire for fire-breathing dragons, enabling them to toast their enemies like marshmallows!

Fairy Secrets

Fairy dust is a fairy's number one favorite tool. No one knows exactly how fairy dust is made, except that it's hand-ground from the purest and freshest ingredients. What is certain is that each batch is custom made for the particular job at hand. So, for example, mending a broken feather would require a much simpler recipe than one for mending a broken heart.

SECRET INGREDIENTS
Fairy Dust No. 3

sliver of bark from an old Oak tree
3 leaves from a Willow tree
1 tsp. pinecone shavings
handful of Peppermint
handful of Parsely
pinch of ground Black Pepper
several Blue Grape seeds
2 drops Lemon juice
3 tsp. Thyme
1 tsp. Nutmeg
smidgeon crushed Sunflower seeds
1 large sprinkle of dried Red Clay
2 large sprinkles of pure White Sand
1 spot from a Ladybug
1 piece of Dragon's tooth
2 oz. of Dewdrop – or 3 oz. of Fog
5 petals from a Red Rose ←
2 tblsp. crushed Clear Quartz
1/2 tsp. Green Tea leaves
1/2 cup Buttercup nectar
1 willing Chipmunk's whisker

Mix to a fine powder and
spread with good intentions.

pink may be substituted for red if absolutely necessary

Some facts about fairies:

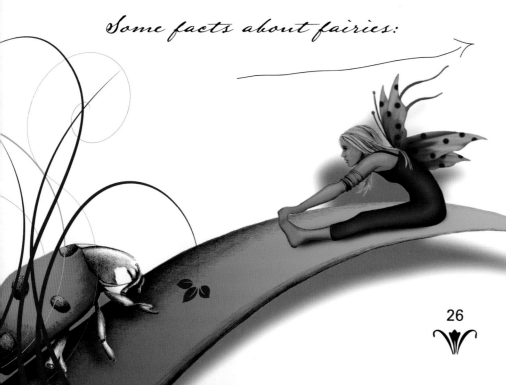

1. Fairies are ageless, timeless and immortal

2. Fairies have superhuman strength

3. Fairies don't need magic wands

4. Fairy tears can turn twigs to stone

5. Fairies weigh practically nothing

6. Fairies work with angels

7. Fairies can stop or speed up time

8. Fairies love to ride horses

WHAT FAIRIES DISLIKE MOST:

Litter
Bullying
Selfishness
Sad plants
Cold iron
Cruelty to animals

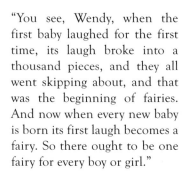

"You see, Wendy, when the first baby laughed for the first time, its laugh broke into a thousand pieces, and they all went skipping about, and that was the beginning of fairies. And now when every new baby is born its first laugh becomes a fairy. So there ought to be one fairy for every boy or girl."

Sir James Matthew Barrie,
Peter Pan

PETER PAN : MYTH & MYSTERY

J.M. Fairie

Lost Boys Publishing

PATRICIA SAXTON

THE BOOK OF MERMAIDS

SHENANIGAN BOOKS

RAINBOW PAINTING AND OTHER FAIRY SECRETS

OBERON / TITANIA PRESS

The Goblin Chronicles

Lord Dragonfairy

MEMOIRS OF TINKERBELL

GEORGE MARGARET

A.C. DOYLE

VOL. IX

Lessons in Enchantment / The Cottingley Cousins

SUGAR PLUM PRESS

LARK SWAIN

THE ADVENTURES OF PUCK FINN

FAERYLAND BOOKS

The True Tales of Harry and Dobby

R. U. Kidding

A Midsummer Night's Dream

WILLIAM SHAKESPEARE

Fairy Language

Fairies can understand every language spoken on the land or sea and can speak easily with all creatures – even you and me.

Of course, they do have their own language which they speak fluently from the day they are born. People find it nearly impossible to learn, but still, you can try.

Here are a few words you'll want to know in case you meet a fairy:

Aguk: *hello.* **Pluptun:** *good-bye.* **Lanlan:** *please.*
She-a-may: *thank you.* **Ah:** *yes.* **Yukyuk:** *no.*

Fairy Medicine

With just a sprinkling of fairy dust, a fairy can make a scrape or cut heal faster, or turn a bad mood into laughter.

With their magical light, fairies can erase worries and fears. When you're feeling restless, their soft and beautiful singing can help you sleep.

But most of the time, fairies won't use these powers unless asked. And since most people are proud, they simply won't ask a fairy for help.

There are rumors that fairies sometimes lure humans back to Fairyland, where people can spend several years and think it was only a day or two.

YOU SHOULD NEVER DISTURB
A CIRCLE OF MUSHROOMS.
THESE ARE CALLED FAIRY
RINGS AND ARE SPECIAL
PLACES WHERE FAIRIES SING
AND DANCE AND CAST THEIR
MAGIC SPELLS.

Celebrations

In their day-to-day lives, fairies are shy and reserved. But if you listen carefully on the first day of spring, summer, fall and winter, you can hear the lively sounds of fairy merrymaking.

On those special days, in the wee hours of the morning, before the moon disappears and the sun rises, fairies the world over spend their time singing, dancing, clapping and laughing.

If you're lucky enough to discover their secret party spot, you'll find a small circle of warm, flattened grass where the fairies sang and danced until the sun came up.

How To Please a Fairy

Who doesn't like a present now and then? Well, fairies are no exception! They'll be tickled pink with peppermints, or tiny bits of fruit or chocolate. And maybe a bright, shiny penny! Sweet treats and glittery things are always fairy favorites.

And because fairies like to sew, buttons, sequins and scraps of fabric also make great gifts. Colorful thread is nice, too – and just a little bit is fine, as fairies can magically turn it into as much as they need.

If you're feeling artistic, find some paper and draw your own fairies. Fairies adore the attention, so your drawings will surely please them. You can also read to them out loud (but not *too* loud!), or sing a favorite song. Fairies just love a good story and will sing along at the drop of a note!

But if you **really** want to please a fairy, you must promise to be kind to all living things – trees and plants, animals, rivers, oceans, *and* other people. Treat them all with courtesy and respect, and, like fairies, be nature's good caretakers.

34

Fairy Creed

As a lifetime guardian of Nature, I, _____, swear to honor and respect every living thing at all times.

In particular, the following plant beings shall be especially revered: Ash, Elder, Hawthorn, Oak and Willow Trees; Apple Blossoms, Bluebells, Buttercups, Clover, Daffodils, Elderberry, Foxglove, Heather, Lavendar, Lilac, Holly, Milkweed, Pansies, Peony, Poppies, Primrose, and Thyme.

Furthermore, all anim
under our care will